D1125546

An Evening With Grandpa

Adventures in Chess Land

By Diana Matlin

Illustrated by S. Chatterjee

DIANA MATLIN

ISBN-10: 0988785013
ISBN-13: 978-0-9887850-1-4

DEDICATION

To Anna, The Chess Princess.

CONTENTS

1. STUCK

Little Annie was upset. Not only did her throat hurt and it was painful to swallow, but the doctor had said to stay home for a couple of days, and now she couldn't go to see The Nutcracker that night. Her parents and her little brother would enjoy the music and beautiful dances, and probably go to her favorite restaurant after the show. But she would have to miss all the fun. And to make it even worse, she had to stay with Grandpa, who would rather sit on the sofa and read his newspaper than play any game with her. Annie felt so miserable, she was ready to cry.

"Annie, please," said her mom, "we can't miss the show tonight. You'll have fun with Grandpa too, you'll see."

"Yeah, right," thought Annie. But she didn't say anything. She felt very tired and sleepy. "I think I'll take a nap," she mumbled instead.

"Good, get some rest and you'll feel better," said her mom, pulling the thick, warm blanket over her and kissing her gently on the forehead.

When Annie woke up, her family had already left and the house was very quiet.

"Grandpa?" called Annie.

"Oh, hi Annie, you're up! Are you feeling any better?" asked Grandpa.

"A little, but I'm bored." replied Annie. "Will you play Chutes and Ladders with me?"

Grandpa thought for a moment. "Maybe next time," he replied.

Annie tried again. "How about Candyland?"

But Grandpa, it seemed, had his mind set on the newspaper. "Let's play the next time I come over."

"Not even checkers?"

Grandpa just shook his head slowly, looking thoughtful.

"Just as I expected," thought Annie, "this is going to be a boring night."

Just then, Grandpa's face lit up and he spoke. "I think I have a good idea. Annie, do you know how to play chess?"

"Not really," Annie replied. "But I do remember there was a magical chess game in one of the Harry Potter movies."

"All right then. Let me tell you a story first," said Grandpa, putting his newspaper aside.

"Is it a fairy tale?" interrupted Annie.

"Not exactly. But we'll make it into one." He paused, noticing Annie's sudden interest. "It's about a little girl who wanted to be a queen very much." He then took a deep breath, as if he was preparing to tell Annie something very special.

"Maybe it won't be as boring as I expected after all," thought Annie. "So what happened to her?" she asked impatiently.

2. THE KINGDOM

"Well, there once was a girl with a funny name, Pawnie, who lived in a faraway Chess kingdom. This kingdom was like no other kingdom you have ever heard of before, because it had two kings and two queens." Grandpa narrowed his gaze. "And what do you think happens when you have two kings and two queens, Annie?" he asked.

"I don't know, do they have a lot of parties?" Annie guessed.

Grandpa chuckled softly. "They do," he answered, "but more importantly, they always fight over who is more powerful."

"But why?" Annie wondered. "Can't they just rule together and have fun parties all the time?"

"See, Annie," continued Grandpa, "The kings always want to have more power, and the queens' job is to help them get it. After that, they can have more parties."

"Hmm." Annie wasn't sure she liked those kings and queens from the story very much.

"So to determine who will be the most powerful king of the land, they all agreed to have a battle with a carefully outlined set of rules. They divided their army into two halves, with white and black uniforms to tell one army from another. The kingdom was not especially large in size, and each king ended up with a total of only two knights, two bishops, two rooks, eight young soldiers and a queen, of course."

Grandpa thought for a minute. "To tell you the truth, Annie, these kings were not very brave. They did not like to fight themselves, and they preferred to stay inside their comfortable castles and tell everybody else what to do instead."

Annie considered this for a moment. "That's not very nice, not when he has an army of people fighting for him. He should be out there fighting with them," she decided.

"Well, Annie, the king was very important, but at the same time he was not very strong himself. If he would get caught on the battlefield, his side would have no chance at all," Grandpa explained.

"Hmm. Well, that's alright, I guess," Annie concluded. "So what happens next?"

"Well, the white king said to his queen, "You are the best queen, you are beautiful and smart. I will let you do anything you consider best for me to win this fight. And when we do, I will buy you a new dress and we will have the biggest and fanciest party in the whole kingdom."

"And new shoes and diamond earrings," added Annie.

"Of course," Grandpa agreed. "The queen was very happy and immediately started planning two things, the party and the battle. She was very excited about the party the king had promised, but she knew that she first needed to think about how to outsmart the other side. And she was indeed a smart lady.

3. THE QUEEN'S PLAN

After some time alone in her chamber, the queen returned to the king and said, "King, your rooks, knights and bishops are very well trained and know what to do. But I think we need to do something about the foot soldiers. They are all young and not as strong as the others. They need to be clever so that they can trick their opponents on the battlefield.

Oh-oh, and all of your soldiers are boys. I think we need to replace some of them with girls. Our opponents will think that girls are weak and easy to defeat, but I will teach them some tricks and they will surprise the other side."

"But Grandpa, girls usually don't like to fight," interrupted Annie.

"That is true," said Grandpa, "but remember, this queen was smart and she came up with the following rule: any girl soldier who could make her way across the field and reach the castle of the other king, would become the princess of the royal family, meaning that when the time came, she would become the new queen.

This was an especially clever idea because the king and queen had no children, and needed an heir to whom they could later pass the throne."

"That is very smart," Annie said. "So did they find any girls then?"

"Something very unexpected happened," continued Grandpa. "So many wanted to become soldiers that the next morning it seemed that all the girls in the kingdom had come out to apply. After some thought and discussion with the king, the queen decided to do something new, something that had never been done before. She decided to give a chance to eight girls, which meant that she would replace all of the boy soldiers. The king was concerned that the girls would not match the boys in size and strength, but the queen was confident in her plan. "I'll teach them what I know and they will outsmart the other side," she assured.

"But Grandpa, you can't have so many princesses in one kingdom," Annie pointed out.

"Yes, that's true. And the queen knew that as well. What she didn't tell them, however, was how difficult it would be to survive in this battle and to get into other castle. They would have to get past all of the opposing kingdom's soldiers, knights, bishops, rooks and most importantly, the powerful other queen. Therefore, it would be impossible for all of them to become princesses."

"She was a smart but a mean queen then," commented Annie.

"She had to be if she wanted to win that fight, otherwise her kingdom would have no chance," replied Grandpa.

"True, but that's still pretty mean," noted Annie. She leaned back on the sofa, trying to judge the queen's actions properly.

"Do you want a snack, Annie?" Grandpa asked suddenly. "Your mom mentioned that you may be hungry after your nap."

"No, let's finish the story first. The snack can wait." Annie replied.

Grandpa chuckled. "All right, Annie, let's finish the story."

4. GETTING READY

The battle was scheduled for the next day. Over the course of the evening everyone remained inside the castle, preparing for the upcoming fight. The knights and the rooks were cleaning their armor and the bishops were practicing their battle strategies. Only the female soldiers were not sure how to prepare.

They reviewed the rules that the queen had told them and went to sleep. But one girl, Pawnie, stayed up. She had never been in any battles, and she felt so worried and scared that she could not fall asleep.

"Maybe I could talk to somebody and at least get some idea of what will happen tomorrow," she thought. So she went around looking to see how the rest of the army was preparing. First, she stopped by the knights and rooks.

"Are you new? We haven't seen you here before. What's your name?" they inquired.

"Pawnie, sirs. Yes, I am new, and I was hoping you would give me some advice for tomorrow."

The knights and rooks felt very proud that somebody was asking them for advice. "Stay where we can protect you," they instructed, continuing, "and remember: you can only move forward but you have to strike diagonally to destroy your opponent. You are stronger than you think, but be careful, and look around you before you move to avoid danger."

"Thank you, sirs, I'll do my best to follow your advice," said Pawnie gratefully, and left them to explore the rest of the castle. Soon she saw the two bishops, who were at that moment arguing passionately among themselves. "Excuse me, can I help you in any way?" asked Pawnie.

"I'm afraid not, you are too young to understand. We are talking about the strategy for tomorrow. It is going to be a very difficult fight," one responded.

"Maybe you have advice for me then? This is going to be my first battle," said Pawnie.

"My goodness, how long have you been a soldier?" asked the other.

"Only since yesterday," answered Pawnie, feeling very nervous.

"Okay, let me give you one piece of advice. At the start of the battle, you can run twice as far as you will be able to later, so it may help you to get ahead," said the first bishop.

"And keep in mind that you can capture other soldiers by moving diagonally!" advised the second.

"Thank you very much, I'll remember that," said Pawnie, and she headed down the corridor. "I should go get some rest," she thought, although she was not sure if she would be able to fall asleep that night.

She was walking back to the room when she heard footsteps. Startled, she turned around and saw none other than the queen herself walking behind her. "Your majesty, it's an honor to see you," Pawnie stuttered, trembling with excitement.

"Good evening, soldier. Are you one of the girls who wants to be a princess?"

"Yes, your majesty, it's my dream to become a queen and I'm ready to do whatever is necessary tomorrow to get to the other castle," Pawnie proclaimed with utmost respect.

"You are very brave, my dear. Remember, although you are not the strongest, you are very smart and you can trick your opponents. Did you learn your magic words?" asked the queen.

"Oh yes, I did, your majesty," she started, "I learned about 'en passant' and..."

"Hush," the queen stopped her. "Somebody may hear you. Good luck to you tomorrow, and remember," she paused, "the fate of this kingdom depends on you." With that, the queen turned around and walked away in the other direction.

"The fate of the kingdom depends on me," repeated Pawnie, feeling very proud and excited to be a part of the battle. "I'll have to get to the other side tomorrow and after that I will become a princess." She then returned to the room where the other girl soldiers were sleeping, crawled into her bed quietly and drifted off to sleep.

5. ROYAL BATTLE

The trumpets sounded early the next morning to announce the beginning of the battle. The soldiers stood lined up in front of the castle, ready to march forward at the king's command. Pawnie stood at the center, directly in front of the queen.

"Begin!" shouted the king.

Pawnie took a deep breath to calm herself down, struggling to focus. "When the battle starts, you can run twice as far as you will be able to later," she remembered, and charged forward. Her heart was pounding when she stopped, and suddenly she heard her name. She turned around and saw the knight that she had talked to the day before. He nodded at her, "Don't worry Pawnie, I'll cover you." Feeling slightly better, she took another cautious step forward. Then, out of nowhere, she heard a loud cry and turned to see an enemy pawn charging toward her with a fierce expression on his face. "Strike diagonally, strike diagonally," she remembered. Pawnie followed the bishop's advice without hesitation and the soldier disappeared as Pawnie slowly caught her breath. She turned around to see where everyone else was and was shocked to see that half of the army was not on the field anymore. Pawnie froze in place.

"Don't look back, Pawnie, you must move forward. You are a soldier and you will reach the other castle," she heard from behind. Pawnie gulped, and took another careful step toward the enemy castle. However, she was not able to see who was addressing her, as at that very moment Pawnie found herself confronted by none other than the black queen.

"And where do you think you're going?" Pawnie looked up and her heart jumped, but she refused to show her fear.

"I am going to your castle," Pawnie said as calmly as she could.

"I don't think so," the queen sneered. "I'm going to take you out of this battle right now."

"No, your highness," came the familiar voice of the white knight from a short distance back. "Not unless you wish to fight with me!"

The black queen glared at Pawnie for what felt like a very long time.

"I'll get you next time," she scoffed, and moved away.

The white knight called, "You are very close, Pawnie, let me ask our rook to help you move ahead. Beware of the queen, she may try to stop you again."

"Thank you, knight," Pawnie replied. She felt very frightened and excited at the same time. The black castle stood just a few steps ahead of her, but Pawnie reminded herself not to be careless and decided to take a few minutes to think. As she struggled to compose her thoughts, Pawnie heard yells and scuffling several files away from her. The white knight and rook were fighting with the black queen. She tried to understand who was winning, but they moved with such speed that Pawnie could not even see what was happening. Just then, she noticed a wide clearing ahead of her. She gasped.

"Pawnie, run forward! You can use a "passed pawn" trick if you move quickly enough!" she heard from behind.

Pawnie did not even turn around to see who was talking. She knew that the consequences of losing even a few seconds could be fatal. She ran faster than she had ever run before, refusing to be distracted or scared into stopping.

Everything around Pawnie faded into a blur.

Then, suddenly, she ran into a wall. "It's the castle, it must be the castle!" Pawnie exclaimed. She turned to see the main staircase and climbed the steps in one breath.

"I am here, I made it!" she rejoiced. Pawnie was so happy that she did not know what to do next.

6. CHECKMATE

Grandpa, Grandpa!" exclaimed Annie. "I know what happened next! The air around Pawnie began to sparkle and she felt something heavy on her head. She touched it and it was a crown, a real royal crown!"

"Oh, Annie, how did you know?" asked Grandpa with a sly smile.

"But Grandpa, you said before it was a fairy tale. That is what should happen in a real fairy tale," Annie explained.

"Well, Annie, you are absolutely correct. The crown made Pawnie feel very powerful, even magical. She ran through the castle prepared to fight anyone who dared get in her way. Pawnie searched every room in the castle, but was disappointed to find they were all empty. At last, she went to the great hall and stepped out onto the balcony. "Pawnie, Pawnie, look down!" came the distant voice of the white queen, "Catch him, he is running away and I can't reach him." Pawnie glanced down and saw the black king, running down the stairs trying to escape. She charged after him, and at that moment Pawnie became convinced that she had acquired some magical powers. Never before had she been able to run so quickly. Pawnie caught up with the king in no time, and with all her might ordered, "Stop, your majesty! The fight is over, you have lost."

"Not so fast, little girl," the king replied, and tried to run in a different direction.

"Did he get away?" Annie asked.

"Remember how I mentioned before that the kings are not very brave?" Grandpa responded.

"I remember," replied Annie.

"They're also not strong, as you know, and can't run fast in their royal costumes. He tried to run, but he was too slow and the white rook cut him off almost immediately. The king then dashed to the other staircase, but stopped in his tracks.

"Checkmate!" Pawnie looked up to see her friend, the bishop, standing on a direct diagonal to the king. The black king looked around in desperation, but there was nowhere else to run. "I can't believe it," he murmured, and put his face in his hands. "I resign," he whispered, sighing heavily and laying his crown upon the floor. "Girl soldiers—who would have thought it would work?"

"It seems we got you this time," the white bishop said. "Good game, Your Highness." Turning to Pawnie, he beamed. "And you, what a brilliant performance! It's almost impossible to believe it's your first time on the battle field."

"Thanks," Pawnie stuttered, suddenly self-conscious and at a loss for words.

"Hooray!" cheered the entire white army. Pawnie blushed. "Now let's bring the news to our king!" they yelled, and ran as fast as they could back to the white castle.

Pawnie wasn't sure if she should go with them, as she was, after all, just a young girl. It seemed like all her powers had drained from her, and all of a sudden she felt very lonely and tired. As she sat on the stairs, Pawnie felt tears coming to her eyes. "It doesn't matter," she thought, "nobody will see me anyway." Just then, however, she heard the approach of the familiar, confident footsteps.

"Pawnie, why are you still here?" inquired the white queen.

"Sorry, your majesty, but I am not sure where I should be or what I should do now," said Pawnie very quietly.

"Oh, how silly..." she chuckled, and Pawnie looked up at her with wide eyes. "Planning the royal ball, with me, of course! Don't you know that it's the queen's job? And I absolutely must have the help of the princess. This will be the grandest ball our kingdom has ever seen, so we must start planning immediately. Come, we have to decide on the dishes, and the music, and take care of the dresses..." The queen continued but Pawnie was not listening anymore. She was so happy!

"Happy as a princess," she thought, and walked faster to keep up.

7. GRANDPA, COME AGAIN!

"Grandpa, that was a nice story, I never knew you could tell fairy tales," Annie said.

"I'm glad you liked it, Annie. I wouldn't be able to come up with it without your help, so I think we can call it our story," Grandpa replied. "And now, while you are eating your snack, I want to show you how to play chess."

It was already dark outside when Annie heard her family pulling into the garage. She ran downstairs, and yelled, "Mom! Dad! I'm playing chess with Grandpa, he told me a fairy tale and taught me how to play. Oh, and I'm feeling better too."

"I'm so glad to hear that you are feeling better," Annie's mom said and smiled. "But wait, did you say that Grandpa told you a fairy tale? I never knew he could do that. He never told me a fairy tale when I was little."

"I guess Annie is just that special," Grandpa grinned. "By the way, she is a very quick learner, I think she'll be good at chess if she keeps going."

"Grandpa, could you teach me more? It's a fun game!" Annie begged.

"It's getting late and you need to get some rest, but I'm sure we can do more next weekend," Grandpa agreed.

"Okay, but don't forget!" Annie replied, and ran upstairs to get ready for bed.

THE END

CPSIA information can be obtained
at www.ICGtesting.com
Printed in the USA
LVOW11s2332201017
553233LV00001B/6/P